Dear Parents:

Congratulations! Your child is taking the first steps on an exciting journey. The destination? Independent reading!

STEP INTO READING® will help your child get there. The program offers five steps to reading success. Each step includes fun stories and colorful art or photographs. In addition to original fiction and books with favorite characters, there are Step into Reading Non-Fiction Readers, Phonics Readers and Boxed Sets, Sticker Readers, and Comic Readers—a complete literacy program with something to interest every child.

Learning to Read, Step by Step!

Ready to Read **Preschool–Kindergarten**
• big type and easy words • rhyme and rhythm • picture clues
For children who know the alphabet and are eager to begin reading.

Reading with Help **Preschool–Grade 1**
• basic vocabulary • short sentences • simple stories
For children who recognize familiar words and sound out new words with help.

Reading on Your Own **Grades 1–3**
• engaging characters • easy-to-follow plots • popular topics
For children who are ready to read on their own.

Reading Paragraphs **Grades 2–3**
• challenging vocabulary • short paragraphs • exciting stories
For newly independent readers who read simple sentences with confidence.

Ready for Chapters **Grades 2–4**
• chapters • longer paragraphs • full-color art
For children who want to take the plunge into chapter books but still like colorful pictures.

STEP INTO READING® is designed to give every child a successful reading experience. The grade levels are only guides; children will progress through the steps at their own speed, developing confidence in their reading.

Remember, a lifetime love of reading starts with a single step!

Step into Reading, Random House, and the Random House colophon are registered trademarks of Penguin Random House LLC.

Visit us on the Web!
StepIntoReading.com
randomhousekids.com

Educators and librarians, for a variety of teaching tools, visit us at RHTeachersLibrarians.com

ISBN 978-1-5247-6982-6 (trade) — ISBN 978-1-5247-6983-3 (lib. bdg.)

Printed in the United States of America   10 9 8 7 6 5 4 3 2 1

3 1526 05007317 7

nickelodeon

TEENAGE MUTANT NINJA TURTLES™

PIZZA PARTY!

illustrated by Patrick Spaziante

Based on the screenplay "Day One, Part One"
by Joshua Sternin and Jeffrey Ventimilia

Random House 🏠 New York

Four mutant turtles live
in the sewers
of New York City.

They are brothers.

They are ninjas.

Donnie can build anything.

Mikey is a joker.

The Turtles leave

the sewers

for the first time.

New York City is
dark and dirty.
The Turtles love it!

The Turtles see

a man on a scooter.

The man is afraid
of the giant Turtles.
He drops a box.

What is in the box?

It is pizza!

"Pizza is the best!"

says Mikey.

The Turtles hear
a scream.

Two men in blue
are grabbing
a girl!

Leo leads the attack!

Raph jumps into action!

Pow!
The man falls
to the ground.

Mikey discovers that the men are really robots!

Small pink aliens are
inside the robots!
They are called
the Kraang.

The Turtles save the girl.

Her name is April O'Neil.

"I know how
we can celebrate,"
Mikey says.

Pizza party!